Clover Time

Adapted by Susan Amerikaner

Based on the episode written by
Craig Gerber and John Kavanaugh

Illustrated by Character Building Studio
and the Disney Storybook Art Team

DISNEP PRESS

Los Angeles • New York

Copyright © 2016 Disney Enterprises, Inc. All rights reserved. Published by Disney Press, an imprint of Disney Book Group. No part of this book may be reproduced or transmitted in any form or by any means, electronic or mechanical, including photocopying, recording, or by any information storage and retrieval system, without written permission from the publisher. For information address Disney Press, 1101 Flower Street, Glendale, California 91201.

First Paperback Edition, January 2016   10 9 8 7 6 5 4 3 2 1
ISBN 978-1-4847-1590-1

FAC-029261-15324

Library of Congress Control Number: 2015944917
Printed in the USA
For more Disney Press fun, visit www.disneybooks.com

It rains and rains.
Rain fills Clover's home.

Clover moves into Sofia's room.

Sofia makes Clover a bed.
He jumps into it.

Feathers fly!
Clover says good night.

Sofia wakes up.
Clover had a snack.

6

Sofia trips on Clover's carrots.
What a mess!

7

An artist will come soon.
He will paint Sofia's picture.

Sofia goes to her room.

She trips over Clover's bed.

The room must look nice
for the artist.

Sofia and Clover paint
pictures of things they love.

Clover makes more of a mess.

Clover snores all night.

Sofia can't sleep.

Sofia tells her friends.

"Make some rules," they say.

Sofia makes rules.

Rule one: NO CARROTS!

Clover hates rules.
Rules are no fun.

A party is fun.

Clover invites his friends.

Clover's friends come
to the party.

They make a big mess!

Sofia is mad.
Clover leaves.

Sofia cleans.

Clover moves in with Rex.

The artist comes.

He cannot make Sofia smile.

He finds Clover's picture.

Clover painted what he loves.
He loves Sofia!

Sofia runs.

Sofia looks for Clover.

She finds him.

"Please come back," she says.

Sofia's best friend is back.

They are both happy!

Clover's home is dry.
He can leave.

"Stay one more night," Sofia says.
Clover has a gift.

Sweet dreams!